To each and every EXPERT – to those parents, grandparents, teachers, librarians, caregivers, child development specialists, paediatricians, nurses, child psychologists, and psychoanalysts who read over and looked over our work, talked to us, taught us, and corrected us over and over again as we created this book for young children. We could not have created this book without you. THANK YOU! – R. H. H.

For Shelley, Yvonne, Nola and Margo
N. B. W.

WALKER BOOKS
AND SUBSIDIARIES
LONDON • BOSTON • SYDNEY • AUCKLAND

First published 2012 by Walker Books Ltd
87 Vauxhall Walk, London SE11 5HJ

2 4 6 8 10 9 7 5 3 1

Text © 2012 Bee Productions, Inc.
Illustrations © 2012 Nadine Bernard Westcott

The right of Robie H. Harris and Nadine Bernard Westcott to be identified as author and illustrator respectively
of this work has been asserted by them in accordance with the Copyright, Designs and Patents Act 1988

This book has been typeset in Berkeley Old Style and Handwriter

Printed and bound in China

British Library Cataloguing in Publication Data:
a catalogue record for this book is available from the British Library

ISBN 978-1-4063-3753-2

www.walker.co.uk

Who's In My Family?
All About Our Families

Robie H. Harris

illustrated by Nadine Bernard Westcott

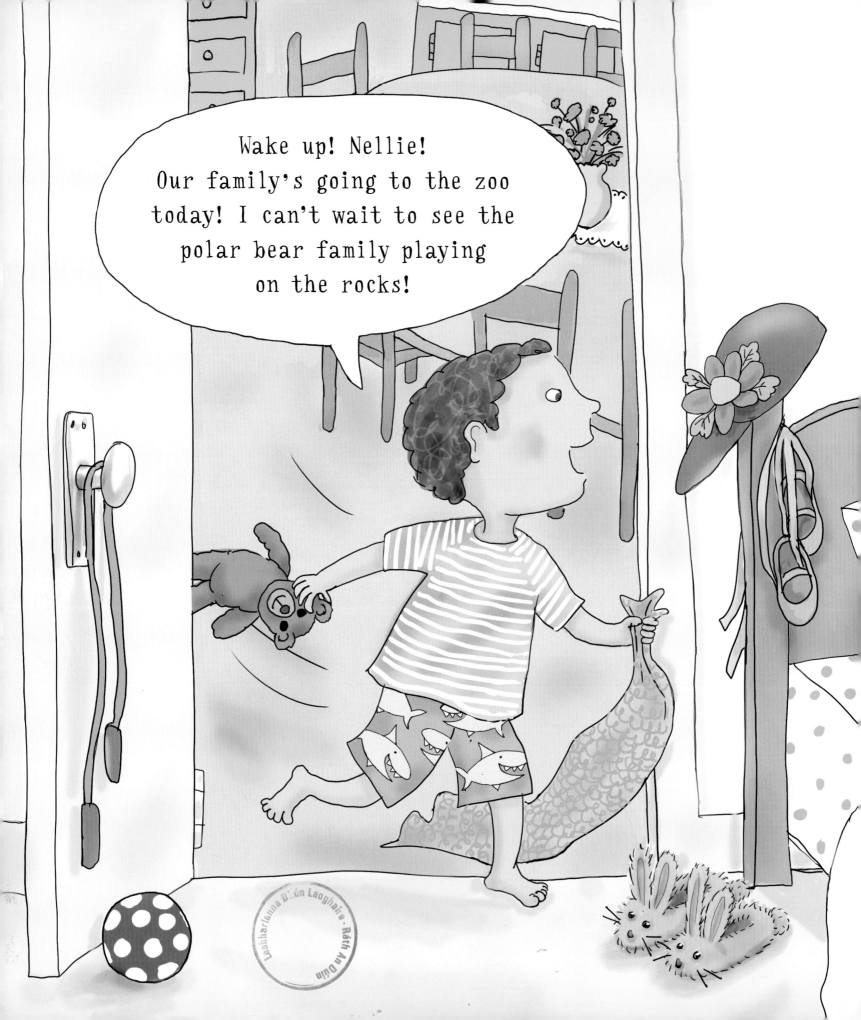

Wherever you live, wherever you go, there are all kinds of families.

Families live in so many different kinds of places.
In cities. In towns. In the countryside.
In flats. In houses. Or on farms.
Families live near lakes. Near rivers. Near oceans.
In the desert. In the mountains. Or on grassy plains.

It's fun to live high up in a flat. I can even see the zoo from here!

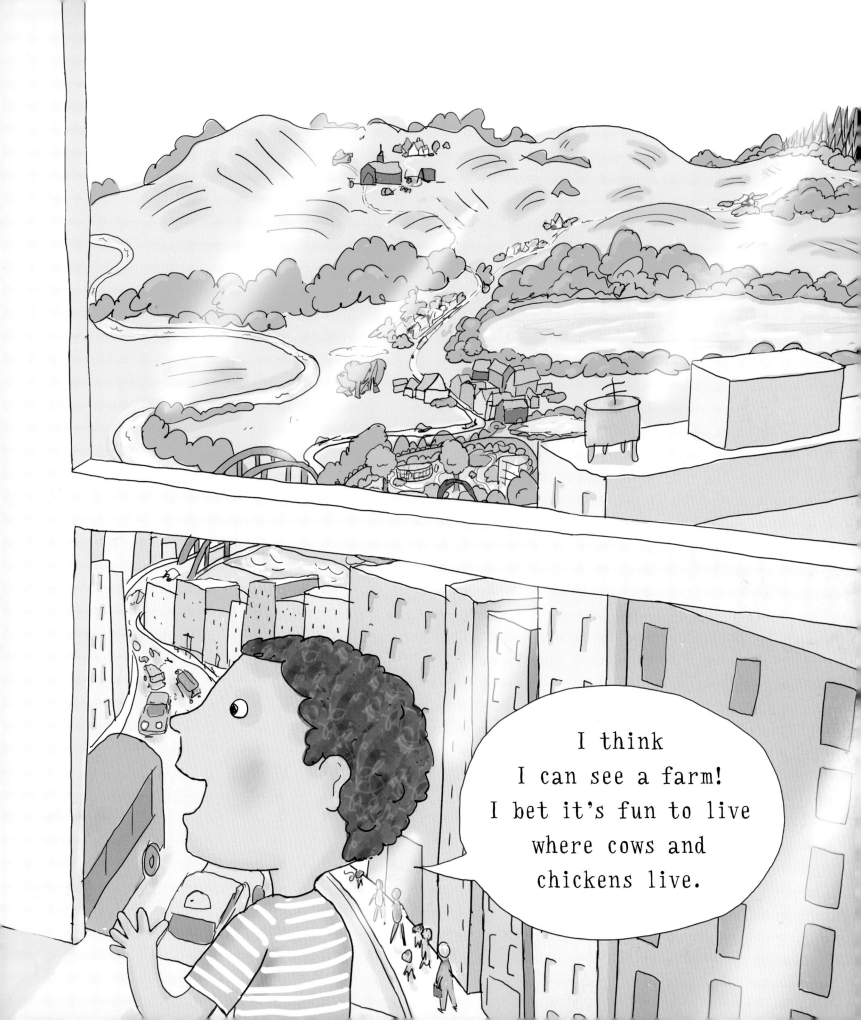

Families eat many different kinds of food for breakfast. Some families eat bacon, eggs and bagels, and drink juice.

Some eat oranges and blueberry pancakes, and drink milk.

Some eat pitta bread, hummus, cucumber and olives.

Some families eat soup, shrimp dumplings and rice.

Some eat raspberries, bananas, muesli and yogurt.

Some eat papaya and burritos, and drink hot chocolate.

Families love being together. Families go to the market, to the library, to the doctor, to the dentist, to the park, to the zoo – and to so many other places together.

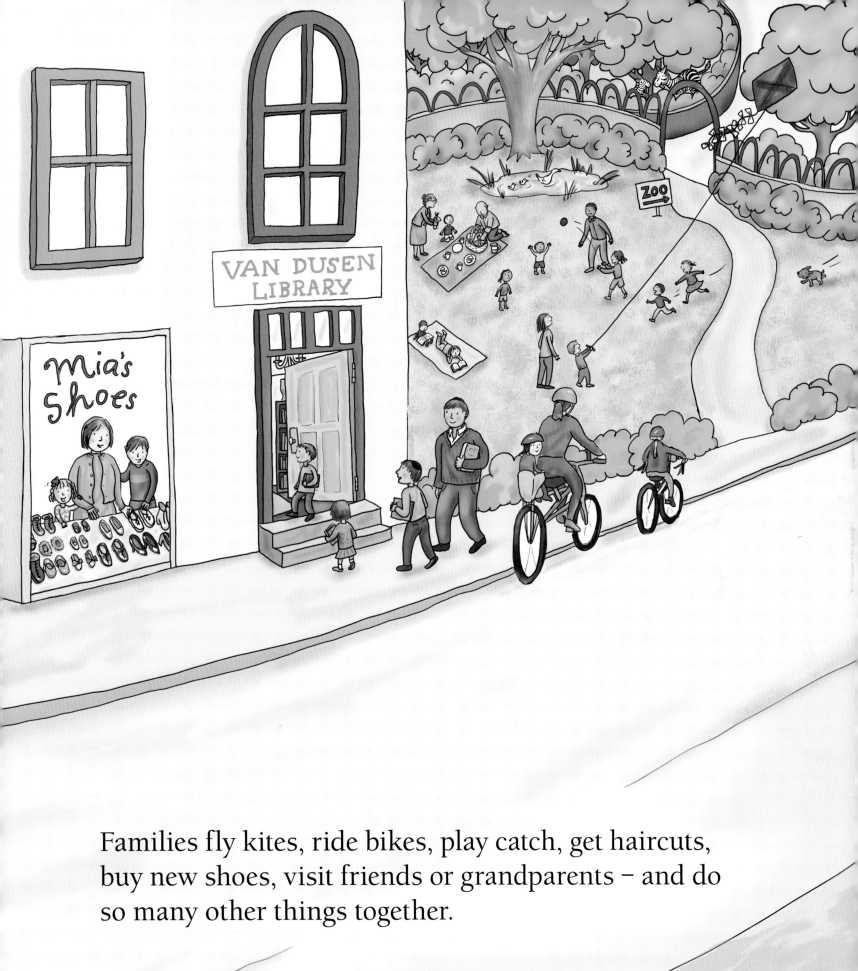

Families fly kites, ride bikes, play catch, get haircuts, buy new shoes, visit friends or grandparents – and do so many other things together.

People families are one kind of family. There are also animal families – squirrel families, polar bear families, sea lion families, zebra families, giraffe families, hippopotamus families, tiger families and so many other kinds of animal families.

Children are born into their families or adopted into their families. And most children live with and grow up in their families. Some families have one child. Some have two children.

Some families have three or four or more children. Some have twins. Some have triplets.

Many families have grown-ups and children in them.
Some families have only grown-ups.
   Some families have a mummy and a daddy. Some have a mummy. Some have a daddy. Some have two mummies. Some have two daddies.

Some children live with their mummy part of the time and with their daddy part of the time.

Some children live with their daddy and a step-parent. Some live with their mummy and a step-parent.

In some families, everybody's hair is the same – mostly wavy or mostly curly or mostly straight. In other families, people have different kinds and different colours of hair.

In some families, everybody has almost the same skin colour. In other families, people have different skin colours. In some families, people's eyes are different colours or different shapes. In other families, people have the same colour eyes or the same shape eyes.

Your eyes, my eyes, Mummy's eyes and Daddy's eyes are all the same colour – brown.

And we all have different shades of skin. Yours is darker and mine is lighter.

Sometimes a grandparent or aunt or uncle lives with a child's family. And some children live in their grandparent's or aunt's or uncle's or foster parent's home.

Parents, sisters, brothers, grandparents, cousins, aunts and uncles can all be part of a child's family. Often, good friends or a pet can be part of a child's family too.

Families have happy times together.

Sometimes, children get a runny nose, a sore throat, a fever or a tummy-ache, or scrape a knee or cut a finger, or just feel bad.

Families help their children feel better and get well.

If I get a tummy-ache, Mummy or Daddy holds me on their lap. And then I feel a lot better.

Parents and children help each other clean up,
put away toys and feed their pets.

After supper,
our puppy licks up
EVERY crumb on the
floor. Our puppy
helps our family
clean up!

Parents help their children have a bath, wash and dry their hair, brush their teeth, and get dressed for bed.

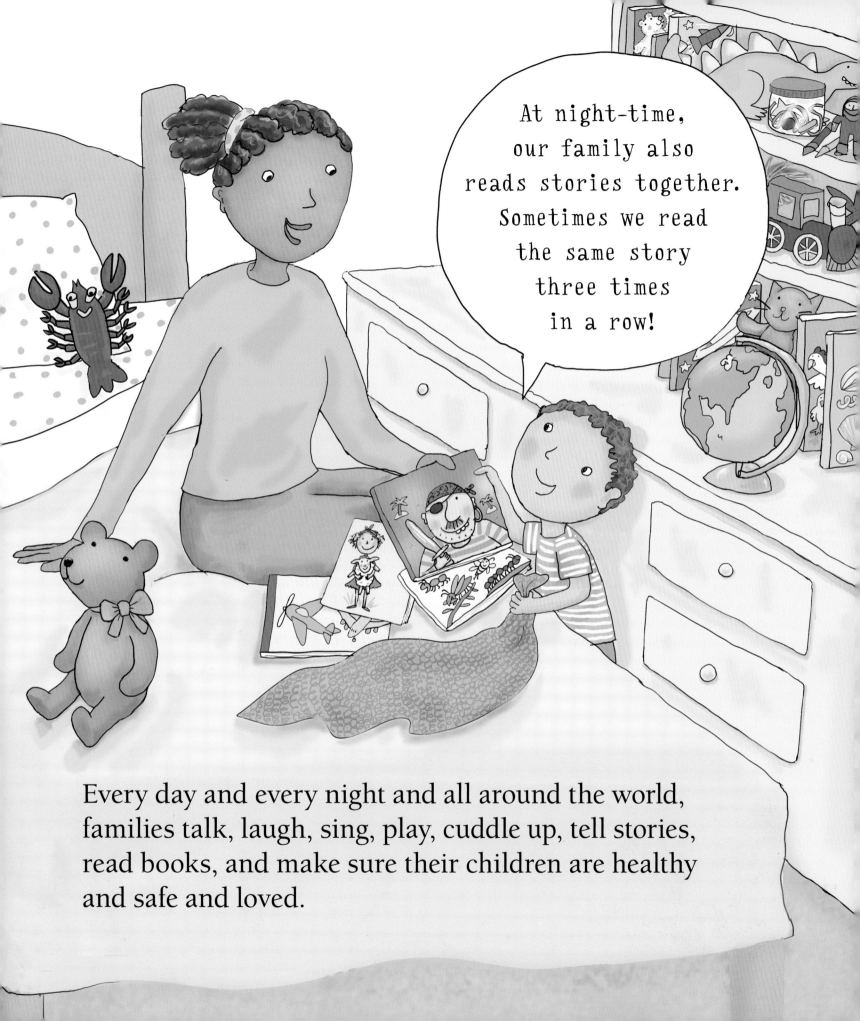

At night-time, our family also reads stories together. Sometimes we read the same story three times in a row!

Every day and every night and all around the world, families talk, laugh, sing, play, cuddle up, tell stories, read books, and make sure their children are healthy and safe and loved.

Most of all, and most of the time, and no matter what –
children and grown-ups and their families really
do love one another!